Ecosystems

Wetlands

Greg Reid

CHELSEA
CLUBHOUSE

An Imprint of Chelsea House Publishers
A Haights Cross Communications Company
Philadelphia

To Mary-Anne, Julian and Damian

This edition first published in 2004 in the United States of America by Chelsea Clubhouse, a division of Chelsea House Publishers and a subsidiary of Haights Cross Communications.

Chelsea Clubhouse
1974 Sproul Road, Suite 400
Broomall, PA 19008-0914

The Chelsea House world wide web address is www.chelseahouse.com

Library of Congress Cataloging-in-Publication Data Applied for.

ISBN 0-7910-7943-0

First published in 2004 by
MACMILLAN EDUCATION AUSTRALIA PTY LTD
627 Chapel Street, South Yarra, Australia, 3141

Associated companies and representatives throughout the world.

Copyright © Greg Reid 2004

Copyright in photographs © individual photographers as credited

Edited by Anna Fern and Miriana Dasovic
Text and cover design by Polar Design
Illustrations and maps by Alan Laver, Shelly Communications
Photo research by Legend Images

Printed in China

Acknowledgments

The author and publisher are grateful to the following for permission to reproduce copyright material:

Cover photograph: a pied oystercatcher in a coastal wetland, courtesy of Pelusey Photography.

J & E Baker/ANTphoto.com.au, p. 28; Cermak/ANTphoto.com.au, p. 17 (bottom left); Martin Harvey/ANTphoto.com.au, p. 14 (top); Silvestris/ANTphoto.com.au, p. 16 (top); John Weigal/ANTphoto.com.au, p. 9 (right); Kathie Atkinson/Auscape International, p. 17 (top right); Ben Cropp/Auscape International, p. 17 (bottom right); Jean-Paul Ferrero/Auscape International, p. 17 (bottom center); Jeff Foott/Auscape International, p. 23; Frank Ingwersen/Auscape International, p. 13 (top left); Wayne Lawler/Auscape International, p. 29; D. Parer & E. Parer-Cook/Auscape International, p. 19 (bottom); Fritz Polking/Auscape International, p. 26; Lynn M. Stone/Auscape International, p. 14 (bottom); Glen Threlfo/Auscape International, p.12; Australian Picture Library/Corbis, pp. 13 (bottom), 24; Corbis Digital Stock, pp. 3 (top & bottom), 7 (bottom), 9 (left), 18, 22, 27, 31, 32; François Gohier Pictures, p. 11 (bottom); Wade Hughes/Lochman Transparencies, p. 13 (top center); Jiri Lochman/Lochman Transparencies, pp. 7 (top), 19 (top), 25 (right); Gunther Schmida/Lochman Transparencies, p. 21 (top); Neil McLeod, p. 20; Pelusey Photography, pp. 5, 6 (main), 16 (bottom), 21 (bottom); Photodisc, pp. 3 (center), 6 (inset), 8, 10, 25 (left), 30 (both); Photolibrary.com/Photo Researchers Inc, p. 13 (top right); The G.R. "Dick" Roberts Photo Library, p. 17 (top left).

Please note
At the time of printing, the Internet addresses appearing in this book were correct. Owing to the dynamic nature of the Internet, however, we cannot guarantee that all these addresses will remain correct.

The author would like to thank Anatta Abrahams, Janine Hanna, Eulalie O'Keefe, Kerry Regan, Marcia Reid.

Contents

When a word is printed in **bold**, you can look up
its meaning in the Glossary on page 31.

How Are Wetlands Formed?

Wetlands occur whenever water gathers on the surface for some time. In some areas, where there is plenty of rainfall, wetlands have a lot of water. In drier areas, some wetlands receive water from underground springs and from occasional storms.

Wetlands are often found in areas where soils and rocks hold water. Fine clay soils stop water from draining away. Wetlands are also found where the slope of the land is flat and water is held in holes. Water in wetlands can either be still or slowly moving. Each wetland is different because they are made in a variety of ways.

Mount Chirripo, Costa Rica. Alpine wetlands are found in mountainous areas with poor drainage.

"Dry" Wetlands

Some wetlands only exist for a short time. They only look like wetlands in the wet season, when there is plenty of water. In the dry season, these wetlands dry out and do not look like wetlands, except for the plants such as swamp grass and bulrushes.

Wetland plants and animals have to **adapt** to these seasonal changes to their habitat. Some animals, such as frogs, turtles, and shrimp, bury themselves under the mud and wait until the wet season.

In Africa, these seasonally dry wetlands are important grazing areas for wild animals, such as buffalo and elephants, and for grazing domestic animals, such as cattle and goats. In the Chad Basin of Nigeria, more than a million people move their animals onto the wetland area in the dry season.

An elephant and her calf grazing on African "dry" wetlands

Ecofact

Buried Alive

The rare western swamp turtle is only found in two small wetlands around Perth, Western Australia. There are only about 200 of these reptiles. They survive summer droughts by burying themselves in the mud and waiting for winter rains.

Western swamp turtle

Types of Wetlands

The two main types of wetlands are inland wetlands and coastal wetlands.

Inland Wetlands

Inland wetlands are found beside rivers, streams, and lakes, or in areas with poor drainage. There is a huge variety of inland wetlands. They include marshes, swamps, **prairie potholes**, floodplains, and bogs. Some inland wetlands are saline, or salty. In the United States, 97 percent of wetlands are inland.

Coastal Wetlands

Coastal wetlands are found around calm protected shores. There is a huge variety of coastal wetlands. They include estuaries, mudflats, lagoons, salt flats, salt marshes, and mangrove forests. They are all affected by the tides. Salt marshes are found in temperate areas of the world, and mangroves are mainly found in tropical areas.

Canada geese, North America

Food Chains

Wetlands have a great variety of plants and animals. Food chains show the feeding relationship between plants and animals in ecosystems. A food chain starts with the Sun, water and nutrients from the water, and soil and **decomposing** plant and animal matter. These basic elements supply energy for plants. The next link in the chain occurs when herbivores and omnivores eat the plants. Herbivores eat only plants, while omnivores eat plants and other animals.

A food chain might continue with carnivores. These animals only eat meat. Carnivores are at the top of the food chain. When any plant or animal in the chain dies, worms and bacteria begin to decompose or break down the matter. The decomposed material returns to the soil and water, where plants take up the nutrients to grow, and the cycle continues.

This pied kingfisher catches fish to eat.

Ecofact

World's Largest Snake

The anaconda is found in wetlands and rivers of Central and South America. It is the top carnivore in its food chain. Anacondas can grow up to 34 feet (11 meters) in length.

Anaconda

Inland Wetlands

There is a huge variety of plants growing in all parts of inland wetlands. Floating plants, such as waterlilies, are common. In tropical areas, papyrus grows in many inland wetlands. In temperate areas, many species of sedge and reed plants, such as cattails, wild rice, and sawgrass, grow in inland wetlands. In some swamps, there are shrubs and large trees, such as white cedars, cypresses, swamp mahoganies, and paperbarks.

Everglades

The Florida Everglades is the world's largest freshwater marshland. It is really a slow-moving river 50 miles (80 kilometers) wide and only about 6 inches (15 centimeters) deep.

A special type of moss, called sphagnum, grows in bogs. Sphagnum traps nutrients, such as insects, on its surface. Other plants, such as willows and alders, die because they do not get enough nutrients. Only a few plants, such as cranberries, cotton sedges, and carnivorous sundews, can survive in this habitat. Over time, the sphagnum moss dies and builds layers of peat on the floor of the bog.

Swamp cypress, from the United States, can grow with the base of their trunks underwater.

Zones in Inland Wetlands

There are four zones of plant life in an inland wetland. Different animals live in each zone. As the plants die and soil washes or blows into the wetland, it starts to fill in naturally. Over time, some wetlands may even change into a forest ecosystem.

Zones in inland wetlands

Emergent zone
Plants such as sedge grasses and cattails grow in shallow water, and emerge above the surface. They have stiff woody stems and help to trap soil.

Floating zone
Plants such as salvinia and duckweed float on the surface of the water with the help of waxy leaves or hairy roots. Waterlilies also grow here and have their roots in the bottom soil.

Submerged zone
Plants such as water milfoil and pondweed grow on the bottom in shallow water.

Shrub and tree zone
Shrubs and trees, such as river red gums, bottlebrush, alders, and willows, grow further back from the edge of the wetland.

Giant Waterlilies

Regalia lilies, from the Amazon Basin in South America, are the world's largest waterlilies. The floating leaf, with its upturned rim, has a diameter of more than 6 feet (2 meters). The flowers are also very large. People eat the seeds of this plant.

Regalia lilies

Inland Wetland Animals

Inland wetland animals have many **adaptations** to help them survive. Some birds, such as jacanas, have long toes to spread their weight as they walk across waterlilies. The basilisk lizard from South America has long back toes with flaps of skin between them. The lizard skids across the surface of the water to escape its enemies.

Beavers, muskrats, ducks, and geese have webbed feet for swimming. The swamp rabbit of North America has wide feet to move easily over wet soil. Merten's water monitors, file snakes, eels, alligators, and crocodiles have flattened tails to help them swim.

Many frogs, such as the water frog, have good **camouflage** to avoid being eaten by predators. However, the corroboree frog, which lives in Australian alpine sphagnum-moss bogs, is black and yellow. Its bright colors tell predators that it is poisonous.

A jacana walks across the waterlilies, holding a chick under each wing.

Inland Wetland Food Chain

Inland wetlands have many plants and animals connected in food chains. Here is an example of a food chain from an inland wetland in North America.

Ecofact

Long-Legged Bird

Herons are found throughout the world. They are long-legged wading birds that feed on fish, shrimp, frogs, and insects. They have keen eyes, long necks, and sharp, slender beaks for catching their prey.

Water milfoil plant gets its energy from the Sun and nutrients from the soil and water.

1 ➡️

Insect larvae, such as a mayfly nymph (herbivore), eats the leaves of the water milfoil plant.

2 ↘️

Inland wetland food chain in North America

6 Water milfoil plant takes up nutrients from the soil and water.

3 Bluegill sunfish (carnivore) eats insect larvae.

5 Snowy egret dies and falls into the wetland, where it is broken down by worms and bacteria (decomposers). The nutrients are returned to the soil and water.

⬅️ **4**

Snowy egret (carnivore) eats the sunfish.

Coastal Wetlands

Coastal wetland plants have adapted to live in saltwater for part of the day. Some plants can live underwater, while others live further away from the sea and can only stand flooding by tides every few weeks. The roots of coastal wetland plants help to bind the soil together.

In temperate salt marshes, plants, such as thrift, sea lavender, and sea milkwort, like to grow away from the sea. Glasswort, eelgrass, and cord grass are the main types of plants that grow in the area flooded each day by the tides.

In tropical areas, there are about 55 species of mangroves. Coastal wetlands are rich breeding, nursery, and feeding grounds for many species of fish, shrimp, shellfish, and crabs.

Ecofact

Killer Crocs

Saltwater crocodiles are the top predator in coastal wetlands in northern Australia and Southeast Asia. They also eat people. After nearly being hunted to extinction, crocodiles in Australia are now protected. Saltwater crocodiles are also raised for their skin and meat.

Saltwater crocodile

Florida Panhandle salt marsh, United States

Zones in a Coastal Mangrove Wetland

Mangrove wetlands are a rich habitat for more than 2,000 species of plants, fish, shrimp, crabs, and shellfish. There are four zones of life in mangrove wetlands in tropical Southeast Asia and northern Australia. Each zone has different mangrove species that are adapted to different **salinity** levels.

Zones in a coastal mangrove wetland

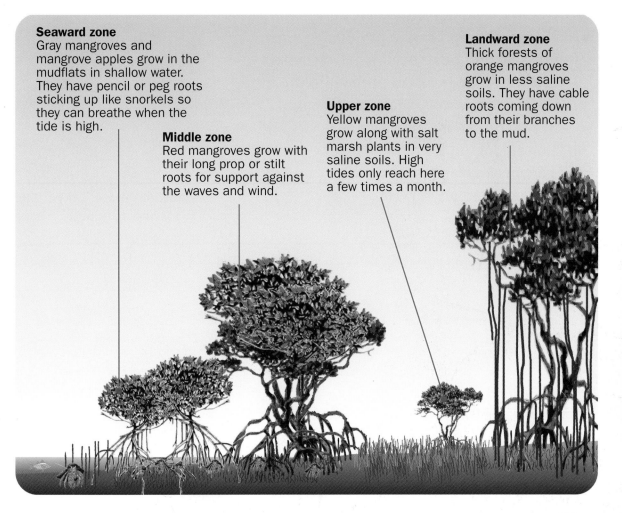

Seaward zone
Gray mangroves and mangrove apples grow in the mudflats in shallow water. They have pencil or peg roots sticking up like snorkels so they can breathe when the tide is high.

Middle zone
Red mangroves grow with their long prop or stilt roots for support against the waves and wind.

Upper zone
Yellow mangroves grow along with salt marsh plants in very saline soils. High tides only reach here a few times a month.

Landward zone
Thick forests of orange mangroves grow in less saline soils. They have cable roots coming down from their branches to the mud.

Coastal Wetland Animals

Coastal wetland animals have made many adaptations to help them survive. Crabs have hard shells and strong arms to defend themselves against enemies. Many animals, such as shellfish, worms, and yabbies, burrow into the mud to escape predators.

Birds have many special adaptations for feeding in different zones of coastal wetlands. In the water, pelicans and terns dive for fish they locate from the air. Avocets sweep their special beak through the mud and water, catching small organisms.

On the land, pied oystercatchers have a special sharp beak to pry open clams, mussels, and other shellfish. Dowitchers use their long beaks to probe into the mud, looking for worms, snails, and shrimp. Ruddy turnstones move small shells and stones looking for hidden small organisms. There is a great variety of ways that wetland animals survive.

Air-Breathing, Climbing Fish

Mudskippers live in mangrove wetlands and mudflats. They can breathe water and air and they use their fins to climb onto branches. Mudskippers can swim underwater, but they prefer to skip across the surface of the water or mud.

Mudskipper

A pied oystercatcher hunting for shellfish on the shore

Coastal Wetland Food Chain

In coastal wetlands, there are many plants and animals connected in food chains. Here is an example of a food chain from the coastal wetlands of tropical northern Australia and Southeast Asia.

Plants such as mangroves get their energy from the Sun and nutrients from the water and mud.

1 → Mangrove plant material decays.

2 →

3 ↓ Shrimp (omnivore) eats the decaying mangrove material.

8 ↗ Mangroves take up nutrients from the water and mud.

7 Saltwater crocodile dies and crabs and shrimp (**scavengers**) and worms and bacteria (decomposers) break it down. Some nutrients are returned to the water and mud.

Coastal wetland food chain in northern Australia and Southeast Asia

4 ← Mangrove jack (carnivore) eats shrimp.

6 ↑

5 ← A barramundi (carnivore) eats the mangrove jack.

Saltwater crocodile (carnivore) eats barramundi.

Ecofact

Fighting Fish

The barramundi, of tropical Australia and Southeast Asia, grows to more than 3.3 feet (1 meter) and weighs more than 110 pounds (50 kilograms). It is very good to eat, and anglers say that it is one of the best fighting fish in the world.

Wetland Flyways

Inland and coastal wetlands have more than one-third of the world's bird species. Some species of waterbirds have adapted to **migrate** from one part of the world to the other to escape the cold winter. Millions of geese, ducks, swans, and cranes breed in wetlands in the Arctic and move south to warmer wetlands in winter. Some shorebirds, such as Eastern curlews and Arctic terns, travel long distances to the Southern Hemisphere.

A flock of geese migrating south to escape the cold Northern Hemisphere winter

On their return journey, the migrating waterbirds often use wetlands along the way as fuel stations. The birds stop over briefly to rest and find food for the long journey ahead. Wetlands are valuable places along the flyways of these migrating waterbirds. If wetlands are cleared, drained, or filled in, it makes it harder for these birds to survive.

Ecofact

Flying South

Geese are well adapted to wetland life, with large webbed feet for swimming, and thick, strong beaks for eating plants. They are strong fliers, and many species, such as the Canada goose, migrate south in winter.

Flood Migration

In Australia, there are many dry salt lakes in the middle of the continent that turn into wetlands after floods. About once or twice a century, after heavy rain, some rivers have enough water to flow into some of these desert lakes. This creates a huge area of ephemeral wetland with its own special food chains.

Millions of brine and shield shrimp hatch from eggs and breed quickly, before the water dries out. Some of Australia's 29 species of desert fish migrate with the floodwaters and feed on the shrimp.

Many waterbirds, such as Australian pelicans, black swans, banded stilts, and silver gulls, arrive from coastal wetlands. They are attracted to these wetlands by the rich food supply. Some birds nest and try to raise chicks. The salt lake wetlands are rich in food, and support many different species while the water lasts.

Lake Eyre is usually a dry salt pan in the South Australian desert. These pelicans will leave when the lake dries up again.

Indigenous Peoples

Indigenous peoples have lived in and around inland and coastal wetlands for many thousands of years. This is because wetlands are very rich habitats for plants and animals. Indigenous people survive in wetlands by fishing, hunting, gathering wild plants, farming, and herding their animals.

An Australian Aboriginal man gathers waterlily roots for food in Arnhem Land, north Australia

Numerous wetland plants, such as wild rice, water chestnuts, lotus roots, and waterlilies, are used as food and medicines. Many wetland animals, such as fish, birds, and frogs, are also used for food. Aboriginal people in northern Australia catch magpie geese, file snakes, northern long-necked turtles, mud crabs, mangrove worms, and many species of fish, such as barramundi. Wetlands are important for the survival of many indigenous peoples and their way of life.

Indigenous Products

Indigenous peoples make many valuable things from their wetlands environment. Wetland plants, such as reeds, flax, palms, and sedges, are used to make brightly colored baskets, bowls, mats, and furniture. Sometimes, these are sold to earn money for the people. Carved wooden animals and implements, such as bowls and dishes, are also popular in Africa and Asia.

Indigenous peoples also make clothes and tools, and build houses and boats, from wetland materials. In Africa and South America, papyrus reeds are used to make boats that transport people around some wetlands. In New Guinea and Southeast Asia, indigenous peoples use dugout canoes made from large trees to move around wetlands. Wetlands supply more than just food and water to indigenous peoples.

A reed boat on Lake Titicaca, Peru

Nipa Palms

Nipa palms are a type of mangrove from Southeast Asia. They supply many useful things for people. The fruit can be eaten after poisons have been removed. The leaves are used for thatching and basket-weaving. The trunks are used for roofing, and the sap is used to make a special drink.

Nipa palms, on the banks of the Mekong River, Vietnam

Wetland Resources

Wetlands provide many valuable resources, such as fresh food and water, for people. Wetlands produce more food than any of the world's ecosystems. Many species of fish, shrimp, crabs, and shellfish feed and breed in swamps, marshes, and estuaries. Fishing industries around the world largely depend on wetlands for their catch. More than 66 percent of the fish caught in the United States and about 75 percent of the fish caught in Australia spend part of their life cycle in coastal wetlands.

Wetlands also provide other wild food supplies, such as ducks, cranberries, sago, and wild rice. In South America, large wetland **rodents** called capybaras are eaten.

Certain wetland trees, such as cedar mangroves, have useful timber for building and making furniture. Some wetland plants, such as marshmallow, are used as medicines. Peat is mined in some bogs and used in gardens and as a fuel. Wetlands provide many sources of food, medicines, and other useful products.

Wetlands are a source of many wild food supplies, such as ducks.

Wetland Recreation and Study

Wetlands are places where people can get close to nature and enjoy fishing, boating, hiking, camping, picnicking, and bird watching. Many of the world's best known wetlands are national parks and wildlife sanctuaries, which are popular with tourists. Examples include the Everglades in the United States, Donana National Park in Spain, Kakadu National Park in Australia, and the Okavango Delta in Botswana.

Because wetlands are halfway between land and water ecosystems, they provide valuable places to study wildlife. There are many **endangered** species in wetlands around the world, such as the marsh deer and giant frog of South America. Scientists and students can study wetland wildlife and food chains and learn more about this ecosystem. Wetlands are valuable recreation and study areas.

Ecofact

Waterbird Hunting

Waterbird hunting is a very popular recreation in many countries. Birds are shot, trapped, and netted. Some countries only allow a special season for hunting. Outside the hunting season, birds can breed without being disturbed.

Birdwatching at the San Francisco Bay Wetlands, California, United States

23

Threats to Wetlands

In the past, wetlands were viewed as smelly, useless wastelands. They were seen as breeding grounds for **parasites**, such as mosquitoes, which carry diseases such as malaria. Many wetlands were cleared, filled, and drained before people realized their value. In some areas, wetlands continue to be destroyed today.

More than half of the world's coastal wetlands have been cleared. Between 30 and 50 percent of wetlands in the United States, excluding Alaska, have been lost, mainly to farming. The Philippines and Indonesia have lost up to 70 percent of their mangrove forests for timber, fuel, and wood pulp. Mangroves are also cleared to create ponds for farming fish and shrimp, and to expand the land for farming and cities. Wetlands are under threat from many human activities.

Ecofact

Threatened Mangroves

Mangrove forests are the most threatened wetland ecosystem in Central and South America and the Caribbean. Many are filled in for towns, industries, and tourist resorts. Others are being cut down for fuelwood, shrimp farms, growing rice, and used for dumping garbage.

These mangroves, in Honduras, have been illegally cleared to make way for a shrimp farm.

Further Threats to Wetlands

Cities, dams, and farm **irrigation** have reduced the water supply to some wetlands. With less water, the wetlands may dry up and the plants and animals die.

In Australia, 80 important wetlands are affected by salinity, which kills plants and animals. The number of wetlands affected by salinity is expected to rise to 130 by the year 2050.

Pollution from sewage, industry, mining, cities, and farming also damages wetlands. Wetlands are able to clean up some chemical pollution, but too much pollution can kill the plants and animals.

The hunting of endangered species and the gathering of their eggs put these animals under threat. Seven of the nine South American crocodile species are endangered through over-hunting for their skins. Over-fishing is also a big problem in many wetlands in Asia. Wetlands are under threat from a variety of sources.

Ecofact

Foreign Invaders

Another threat to wetlands is when foreign plants and animals are introduced. Water hyacinth and salvinia from South America, tilapia fish from Africa, and the cane toad from Central and South America have become serious pests in many wetlands around the world.

Salvinia is choking this wetland in Kakadu, northern Australia.

Pollution kills wetland plants and animals.

Effects of Damaging Wetlands

Wetlands provide many valuable services to people. They are called "nature's kidneys," because they dilute, filter, and settle out pollutants, nutrients, and sediment. If wetlands are cleared or drained, the quality of water will get worse.

Wetlands act like giant sponges and slow down floodwaters. When they are cleared or filled in, flooding becomes worse, and lives and property may be lost. Coastal wetlands protect the land from **erosion** by storm waves. If wetlands are removed, the land may be washed away. Expensive coastal protection walls may then need to be built.

Wetlands, especially bogs, store carbon and help prevent global warming. The burning of wetland timber and peat from bogs releases carbon dioxide into the atmosphere and adds to global warming. Wetlands need to be protected so they can continue to provide their valuable services.

One of the world's largest wetlands is Pantanal, in Brazil.

Ecofact

Groundwater Feeders

Wetlands also feed water into groundwater supplies. More than 50 percent of the population of the United States depends on groundwater for their water supplies. Without wetlands, there will be less groundwater.

Endangered Animals

When wetlands are damaged, the habitat for many species of endangered animals is threatened. Unless wetlands are protected, endangered species may become extinct. They will have nowhere else to live. Some wetland animals, such as the dwarf hutia, a small rodent that lived only in the Zapata Swamp in Cuba, are already extinct.

In Asia, many large endangered animals live in wetlands. These include the Bengal tiger, Sumatran tiger, Indian one-horned rhinoceros, Sumatran two-horned rhinoceros, swamp deer, and pygmy hog. **Poaching** of these endangered animals still occurs for their meat, skin, or horns. If these animals are to survive, their wetland habitat needs to be protected.

Damage to wetlands threatens the extinction of many endangered animals, such as the Bengal tiger in Asian wetlands.

Protecting Wetlands

More laws are needed to prevent wetlands from being destroyed. At present, only a small amount of the world's wetlands are protected in national parks and wildlife reserves. This has increased in recent years, as people realize how important wetlands are to life on Earth.

In 1971, an international wetlands agreement, called the Ramsar Convention on Wetlands of International Importance, was signed in Ramsar, Iran. The Convention aims to help countries protect wetlands and their resources wisely. It also helps countries to cooperate in wetland conservation.

By the start of 2003, a total of 133 countries had signed the Ramsar Convention. There were 1,229 wetland sites on the Ramsar List of Wetlands of International Importance. These protected areas covered an area of 409,000 square miles (105.9 million hectares). However, more wetlands need to be protected so this ecosystem is not endangered.

Kakadu National Park, in northern Australia, is a World Heritage Area.

World Heritage Areas

The United Nations Educational, Scientific and Cultural Organisation (UNESCO) lists natural or cultural sites that are of great importance to the world. The countries where these World Heritage Areas are found must look after these sites. Some wetlands, such as Kakadu National Park in northern Australia, are protected in World Heritage Areas and are very popular with ecotourists.

Conservation Groups and Ecotourism

International conservation groups like the World Wildlife Fund (WWF) help protect wetlands. They let people know about the problems faced by wetlands. Some conservation groups buy land for wetland reserves. They also pressure governments to set up reserves and to pass laws to protect wetland plants and animals. Through the efforts of these groups, international agreements have been made to stop the illegal trade in endangered animals.

Ecotourism is when visitors pay to see the beauty of a natural ecosystem. People visit wetlands to see the wildlife and natural beauty. Ecotourism does not cause much disturbance to the wetlands, and governments and local people can earn more money from people visiting wetlands than from clearing them. Indigenous people can become guides, showing visitors wetland plants and animals. Ecotourism can help protect some valuable wetlands for the future.

Wetland Ecotourism

Almost every country around the world now has wetland ecotourism tours and information centers. Ecotourists can learn first-hand about unique wetlands and their importance as ecosystems.

A large ecotourism industry is based around the wetlands of Kakadu National Park, in Australia.

How to Save Wetlands

We can all work to save wetlands. You can learn more about the importance of wetlands to the world. Join a conservation group and let others know about the threats to wetlands. Join a group that looks after local wetlands. Do not litter or put oils, paints, and chemicals in the drain. Let people know about World Wetlands Day on February second each year. Write to the government and ask them to help save the world's wetlands. The governments of rich countries can help poor countries protect their wetlands for the good of everyone.

ecosystems

The following web sites give more information on wetlands.

Coastal wetlands
http://ssec.org.au/towra/html/coastal_wetlands.html

Ecosystems: wetlands
http://www.stemnet.nf.ca/CITE/ecowetlands.htm

Greenwings
http://www.greenwing.org/greenwings/home2.htm

Swamps
http://www.enchantedlearning.com/biomes/swamp/swamp.shtml

Wetlands
http://mbgnet.mobot.org/fresh/wetlands/

Wetlands: wonderlands, not wastelands
http://www.dnr.state.wi.us/org/caer/ce/eek/nature/habitat/wetland1.htm

Glossary

adapt	the special way in which plants and animals change in order to survive
adaptations	changes that help plants and animals survive in an environment
amphibian	an animal that can live on land and in water
bogs	wetlands fed by rainwater which are rich in decaying plant material
brackish	a mixture of freshwater and saltwater
camouflage	when an animal's color or shape help it to blend into the background
decomposing	breaking down
endangered	in danger of becoming extinct
erosion	the removal of soil and rocks by wind, water, or ice
habitat	the environment where organisms live
indigenous peoples	groups of people who first lived in a place, whose traditional ways help them to survive in that place
irrigation	a system of pipes or channels that brings water to crops
mammals	a group of animals that have hair or fur, warm blood, a large brain, and feed their young milk
migrate	to move from one area to another instead of staying in one spot
parasites	small organisms that feed off another animal
poaching	illegal hunting of animals
prairie potholes	wetland areas in the prairie grasslands of North America
rodents	small mammals with sharp front teeth
salinity	salt in the soil or water
scavengers	animals that live off dead animals
species	types of plants and animals

Index